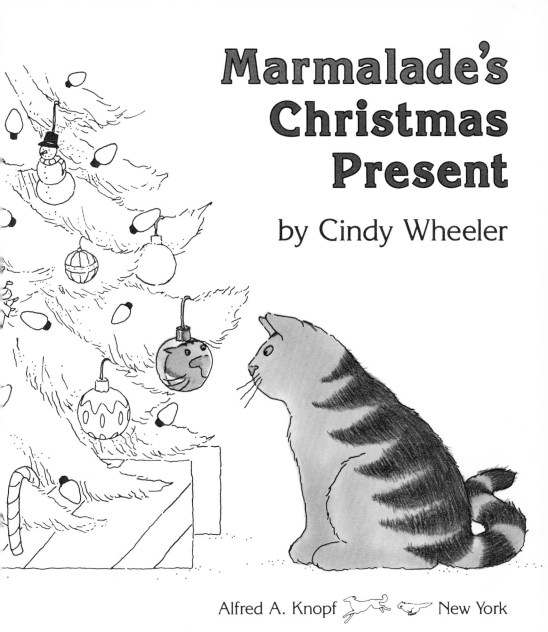

Marmalade's Christmas Present

by Cindy Wheeler

Alfred A. Knopf New York

FOR "KITTY RAT" & "RABBIT"

This is a Borzoi Book Published by Alfred A. Knopf, Inc.

Copyright © 1984 by Cindy Wheeler

All rights reserved under International and Pan-American
Copyright Conventions. Published in the United States
by Alfred A. Knopf, Inc., New York, and simultaneously in
Canada by Random House of Canada Limited, Toronto.
Distributed by Random House, Inc., New York.
Manufactured in the United States of America

Library of Congress Cataloging in Publication Data
Wheeler, Cindy. Marmalade's Christmas present.
Summary: Marmalade the cat finds a very lively surprise
waiting for him under the tree on Christmas morning.
[1. Cats—Fiction.   2. Christmas—Fiction] I. Title.
PZ7.W5593Man 1984   [E]   83-24406
ISBN 0-394-86794-7   ISBN 0-394-96794-1 (lib. bdg.)

Today is special.

There is a tree in the room.

There are boxes under the tree.

Marmalade wants breakfast,

but everyone is busy.

This one is for Marmalade!

"Marmalade, this is Sassafras."

Sassafras chases her tail.

She chases Marmalade's tail, too.

Sassafras finds a place to hide.

What's *that*?

Marmalade gets some milk.

Sassafras likes milk, too.

Sassafras likes to climb trees.

She doesn't know the way down,

but Marmalade does.

Sassafras loves Marmalade.

Cindy Wheeler grew up in Alabama, Virginia, and North Carolina. After receiving a B.F.A. degree from Auburn University, Ms. Wheeler worked for a bookseller and for a publisher. Now she devotes full time to writing and illustrating children's books.

Ms. Wheeler lives in Cold Spring, New York, with her husband, one black cat, and one white kitten.